THE STORY of the WOLF

Written by James Carter

T0327770

CONTENTS

Collins

INTRODUCTION: AN OLD REPUTATION

The wolf has to be one of the most beautiful and bewitching yet misunderstood creatures on Earth. Despite its terrible reputation for many hundreds of years, this so-called "big bad wolf" is at much greater risk from humans than we are from wolves. In the act of clearing the wild, we have slaughtered several million wolves worldwide.

So is the wolf really a devious beast that is a danger to humanity? Well, actually, the opposite is true. By nature, the wolf is a shy creature. Unless **provoked**, it will always choose to keep well away from people.

We are far more likely to be harmed by dogs than by wolves, as wolves never choose to hurt us unless directly threatened. They avoid confrontation with any large animal, as they need to save their energy for hunting and survival. However, dogs have been bred to live with people over many centuries, so they no longer fear us. As a result, on rare occasions dogs may have the confidence to attack humans.

The wolf's story is a fascinating one, telling of its evolution, its survival in the wild and its ability to adapt to extreme conditions over many thousands of years. It's a story that tells us as much about humans as about the wolf itself.

THE CANID FAMILY

Unlikely as it may seem, wolves and humans have a lot in common. We are both **mammals** that adapt well to a wide variety of **habitats** and **climates**. We are both clever and competitive. We are social and intelligent creatures. We have individual personalities, we communicate well and stake out our own territories. As parents, we take our roles very seriously and put much time into educating our young. And we are both playful, curious and keen to learn.

dingo

fox

coyote

Grey wolf

However, humans are **primates** and wolves are part of the **canid** family – which includes foxes, **coyotes**, dingoes, jackals and pet dogs. Canids are found on every continent except Antarctica, and all members share the same features – thick, bushy tails, strong teeth and pointed noses. What's more, all canids are highly social beings that live and function best in groups.

There are two main species of wolf – the better known and more widespread Grey wolf and the Red wolf from the south-eastern part of North America. There is also a third species – the Ethiopian wolf from North Africa.

All these animals are part of the canid family.

pet Collie dog

jackal

Red wolf

RED WOLVES AND ETHIOPIAN WOLVES

The Red wolf is smaller than its grey cousin, thinner and more fox-like in appearance. The Ethiopian wolf is smaller than a Grey wolf too – similar in size to a coyote, though it has red and white fur and a pointed muzzle.

   The Ethiopian wolf is one of the rarest canids in the world. Both Red and Ethiopian wolves live on smaller prey than their grey relation – mostly **rodents**. They are both endangered species.

Red wolf

Ethiopian wolf

GREY WOLVES

The Grey wolf is not only the largest of all the wild canids, it's also the biggest and by far the most common of the three wolf species. Once, Grey wolves were found all over the northern **hemisphere** – in North America, Europe and Asia. The current Grey wolf numbers – estimated at around 200,000 worldwide – are low compared with what they once were.

Wolf fact

There are five main types of Grey wolf – Arctic wolf, Northwestern wolf, Great Plains wolf, Mexican wolf and Eastern Timber wolf.

Arctic wolf

Eastern Timber wolf

Great Plains wolf

North Western wolf

Mexican wolf

THE WOLF PHYSIQUE

To help it cope with the harsh winters in northern lands, the Grey wolf has a warm, dual-layered coat, which can be coloured anything from white to silver-grey to grey-brown to black. As spring appears, the wolf will shed great tufts of its undercoat.

SURVIVAL FEATURES

Wolves have the ideal features for surviving and communicating in difficult **terrain** and over long distances. They have fine hearing, excellent sight, and some 200 million specialised cells in their snouts which give them a great sense of smell, and help them sniff out their prey. For devouring meat, wolves have a rough tongue and 42 sharp teeth set into their mighty jaws.

So that they can run at speed over snow, wolves spread their slightly-webbed toes, which stop them slipping or sinking in. As they move, wolves may walk, trot on their toes or gallop. Wolves can often run at speeds of up to 56 kilometres per hour, and can keep this up for many hours.

A closer look

The Grey wolf is close in size to a large dog such as a German Shepherd, though it has longer legs and bigger feet. An adult male Grey wolf can be anything up to 1.5 metres in length, and may weigh up to 60 kilograms. The Grey wolf is also often referred to by its scientific name, *Canis lupus*.

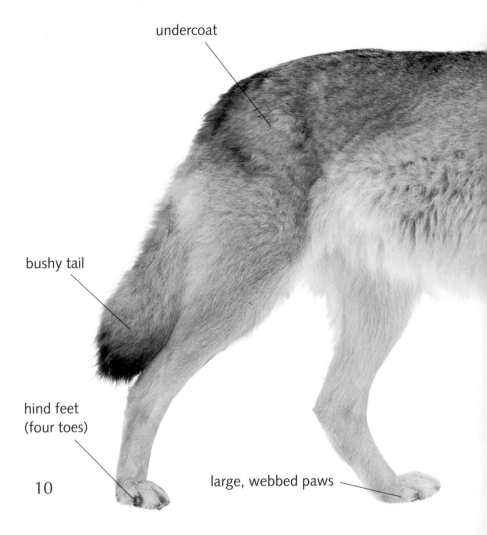

undercoat

bushy tail

hind feet
(four toes)

large, webbed paws

The long-limbed skeleton of the Grey wolf enables it to be agile and to run at speed over great distances.

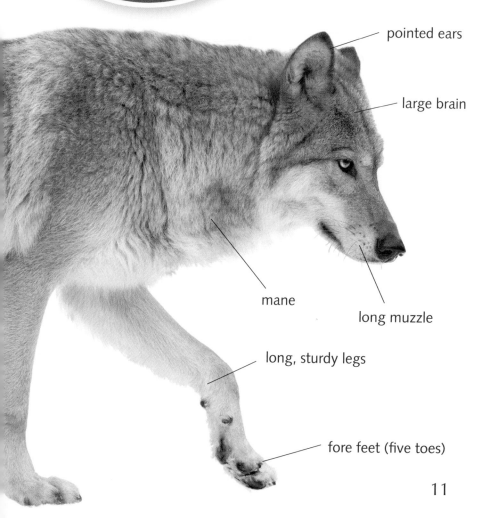

pointed ears

large brain

mane

long muzzle

long, sturdy legs

fore feet (five toes)

11

THE WOLF PACK

A SENSE OF FAMILY

If you ever get the chance to watch a family or "pack" of wolves in the wild, you'll see them for the caring and affectionate creatures that they are. Like humans, wolves have a strong sense of family and community.

Wolf packs often contain ten to 15 wolves, though packs of over 30 animals have sometimes been known. There's one pair of parent wolves in each pack, and these will be the only two that mate.

The term "lone wolf" is misleading, as wolves survive by living together. If wolves are ever seen alone, they are probably looking for their pack, or seeking others to bond with and form a brand new pack. However, wolves will fight those from other packs for food or territory.

Like humans – and other mammals such as whales and elephants – wolves care for their sick and elderly. The death of a parent can have a huge impact on the pack, and wolves grieve for their lost ones. When grieving, just like us, they can become withdrawn for a while, losing their playful spirit, and it can take time for them to become their usual selves once again.

Wolf pups

The breeding season is between January and May, and there are normally four to six pups in a litter. The female will **wean** her young after eight to ten weeks, and after that, the pups will beg for food from any adult wolf.

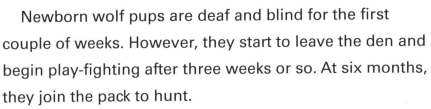

Newborn wolf pups are deaf and blind for the first couple of weeks. However, they start to leave the den and begin play-fighting after three weeks or so. At six months, they join the pack to hunt.

Most wolf pups die if there isn't enough food – yet those few that do survive into adulthood live up to eight years. In **captivity**, they can live as long as 20 years, as food is provided, there are no threats or dangers, and the climate is gentler.

COPING WITH DANGERS

What kills wolves? The dangers include disease, starvation and being injured by their prey when hunting. Humans are also a major threat to wolves; they may be shot by hunters – not always legally. They can also be killed by speeding traffic, because at times wolves mark out their territories along the edges of busy roads.

Wolf fact

In *The Jungle Book*, the author Rudyard Kipling included the poem "The Law of the Jungle" – which has the classic lines: "the strength of the pack is the wolf, and the strength of the wolf is the pack".

Mowgli with the wolf mother in Disney's *The Jungle Book*

WOLF COMMUNICATION

One common myth is that wolves are enchanted by the moon. There are well-known tales of people shape-shifting into werewolves at a full moon, but these are only stories. And it's just a coincidence that wolves often howl when there's a moon in the night sky. In fact, wolves can howl at any time of day or night.

Another myth is that the wolf's main call is a howl. Actually, more commonly they moan, whine, bark, snarl, yelp, whimper or cry. Howling is basically just a good way of communicating across long distances. Usually, howling seems to express bonding with others. Wolves howl when they need help, when grieving a lost pack member, to reunite the pack or to celebrate victory. Sometimes howling is a means of telling others to keep away.

Just as we might use gestures when we speak – or even hug or hold hands – wolves communicate physically too. They wag their tails, lick, sniff or nuzzle each other's faces – as well as touch chins, crouch and roll over.

Scenting a territory with dung or urine is yet another form of wolf communication.

Just like cats and dogs, wolves show certain facial and physical expressions when fighting – they bare their teeth, snarl and hunch their shoulders. Yet a happy wolf, much like a dog, will stick its tongue out and extend its ears.

Hunting and diet

Working as a pack

Wolves are top predators, brave and skilful enough to hunt prey bigger than themselves. It helps that wolves commonly hunt in packs, allowing them to track down a larger creature for many hours, at great speeds and over long distances, if required. On the hunt, the pack will work closely together as a team, and younger members may simply watch – observing and learning for future hunts. Wolves may well spend up to one third of their lives searching for food.

A pack of wolves will seek out a moose, bison or elk, though a single wolf may hunt for a smaller animal – like a hare, beaver or fish. A pack can chase a herd or a single animal for many miles, and wolves can even be seriously hurt themselves. Some of the wolves may run around the prey to disturb or confuse it, whilst another may attack from behind, striking at the flesh with its teeth. A loss of blood may well weaken the animal, slowing it down, and allowing the whole pack to attack and finally feed.

How and what wolves eat

The speed and **agility** of the wolf – as well as its powerful jaws and sharp teeth – are all essential for attacking prey. Wolves will always aim to single out the younger, older or weaker victims, as this enables them to save their strength and avoid being injured.

Generally, wolves seem to prefer to eat the meat of **herbivores**, and they are also known to eat fruit and vegetation to give them the extra **nutrition** they need. Like dogs, they will eat grass when their stomachs are upset. Wolves rarely drink water as they get enough liquid from the meat that they eat, though they may lick dew off grass, or occasionally cool down by lapping up water from a puddle, lake or stream.

In the wild, adult wolves need to eat around three kilograms of food per day in order to be healthy, though they can survive on about one kilogram per day if they have to. If food is scarce, adult wolves can exist for days or even weeks without eating anything.

Wolf fact

Wolves eat as much of their prey as possible, even the bones.

HOW WOLVES AND DOGS EVOLVED

All canids are believed to have evolved from a group of prehistoric carnivores known as miacids, that lived between 62 and 33 million years ago. Recent research suggests that several different types of wolf-like canids appeared about two to three million years ago, and these eventually evolved into the wolves we know today.

The Grey wolf has been around for a million years or so now, and it most likely came from Asia.

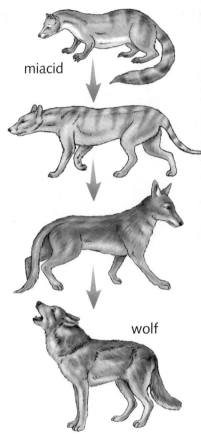

miacid

wolf

Wolf fact

The Dire wolf was an early species of wolf in North America that died out around the end of the last Ice Age, around 10,000 to 15,000 years ago. It's thought that the Dire wolf became extinct because of climate change and lack of food. It would have competed with Sabre-toothed tigers for prey.

WOLVES LIVING ALONGSIDE PEOPLE

A number of scientists believe that some wolves may have begun to live alongside people as far back as 35,000 to 40,000 years ago.

When prey became scarce for wolves, it's thought that they began to rely on waste food such as bones and scraps left outside human settlements.

Some wolves gradually became so used to being close to people that they integrated into our world, living and hunting alongside early humans.

Training and breeding dogs

Modern dogs and wolves have both evolved from a wolf-like common ancestor. People eventually discovered they could train the cubs of these wolf-like creatures to become **domesticated**. They then began to select the calmer and less aggressive cubs to breed from. Over a long period of time, the **descendants** of those cubs became domestic dogs. All dogs nowadays look and behave the way they do as a direct result of the way humans have bred them.

People began to domesticate dogs around 30,000 years ago.

It's no accident that wolves are two to three times stronger than domestic dogs, as humans have deliberately bred dogs to be safer to live with and easier to control than wolves.

Wolf fact

Wolves in the wild rely on adrenaline – an energy-providing natural chemical in their bloodstream – to help them hunt and run at high speed. Dogs don't have or need the same high adrenaline levels.

WILD AND TAME

From pit bulls to pugs to poodles, all pet dogs gradually began evolving from their wolf-like ancestors around 30,000 to 40,000 years ago. To be wild like the wolf is to be the opposite of a pet – a wolf is independent, a creature that doesn't need humans. However, after many centuries of living with people, pets completely rely upon us for survival.

TAMING THE WILD

We've tamed wild animals for many reasons – for company, to guard our homes, to kill pests such as mice and rats, to help us hunt and even to raise as our own food.

With the right conditions, and over many generations, dogs' wild wolf-like ancestors became domestic creatures – but many other wild beasts can't be tamed at all, due to their sizes, their naturally aggressive or carnivorous natures or their basic physical needs. It also makes a difference whether they are social or solitary animals, as social animals are much easier to tame. Fancy a shark in your bath? Mmm ... maybe not!

The boy and the wolf

Deep in the Chauvet Cave, in France, there are magnificent cave paintings of animals on the walls. These date back to around 32,000 years ago, and show creatures common then in Europe – such as lions, rhinos and wild horses. There are also prints preserved in the mud floor that are more recent, from around 26,000 years ago. Scientists believe they are the footprints of an eight-year-old boy and the paw prints of a wolf. From this evidence, it would appear that the boy and the wolf were travelling together through the cave. The boy was holding a flaming torch. But were they companions? Had the boy travelled there to view the paintings? We can only guess.

Wolves and civilisation
Farms, villages and towns

Humans began to mistrust wolves when we moved away from being hunter-gatherers and started to grow our own food on farms, around 11,000 years ago.

Over time, we began to build permanent homes in villages, towns and cities. More than any other animal species, humans have dramatically altered the world. In creating our modern civilisation, we've changed the natural environment with our buildings, roads, transport systems and industries.

Most significantly for wolves, we destroyed large forested areas to create farmland. What use were forests, when fields could be used for building on, for growing crops and for farming? As a result, wolves lost much of their natural forest habitat as well as their prey, such as deer and elk – and all due to human activity. Therefore, wolves had little choice but to venture into farms to seek out sheep, cows and goats in order to feed. As a result, farmers and hunters wanted revenge on wolves. To keep their animals safe, they also killed off other predators such as **lynx**, **cougars** and coyotes.

TOP PREDATORS

It's believed that the last wild wolf in the British Isles was seen in Scotland in the 17th century. But in the Dark and Middle Ages, when much of England was still forested, there were actually more wolves in the UK than people.

At that time, wolves were amongst Britain's top natural predators. The wolf would have been an occasional threat to farm animals, when their usual prey was scarce. As a result, the wolf became the villain of many of the oral folk tales that began in these farming communities. The bad reputation that the wolf gained through these stories stuck, eventually giving us the cliché of the "big bad wolf" which still remains today.

A scene from the folk tale *Little Red Riding Hood*

Now that wolves have disappeared from the wild in Britain, smaller carnivorous predators such as foxes, badgers, otters and Scottish wildcats dominate Britain's natural environment.

fox

badger

Scottish wildcat

otter

Wolf fact

Wolves aren't the only large carnivorous predators to have lived in Britain. Bears and lynx were also once common, as were wild boars. In Britain, bears are thought to have died out during Roman times, and lynx became extinct there in around 500 CE.

lynx

Eurasian brown bear

WOLVES AS VICTIMS

Once there were many millions of wolves globally, and they were the most common predatorial mammal in the world. For hundreds of years after the rise of farming, vast numbers of Grey wolves were killed throughout Europe. However, the greatest large-scale destruction of wolves took place between the 1600 and 1900s, when European settlers came to North America.

During that time, the settlers slaughtered some two million wolves – all of which were trapped, hunted down, shot or poisoned. People used domestic dogs to help them hunt these creatures down.

Hunters with slaughtered wolves

Why this devastation? Because the settlers wanted to build farms that were safe from threats and free from natural predators, and because many of them were superstitious and wrongly considered the wolf to be a force for evil. There was such hatred towards wolves that some were even tortured.

The **indigenous** peoples of North America looked on with horror. To them, the wolf was a creature to be respected, and it remains a key figure in Native American culture and religions to this day.

In some Native American legends, wolves have healing powers and even save humans from a great flood. Dempsey Bob, from the Wolf Clan of the First Nation Canadians, stresses: "To us, the wolf is very important – his characteristics, his strength, his knowledge of the land."

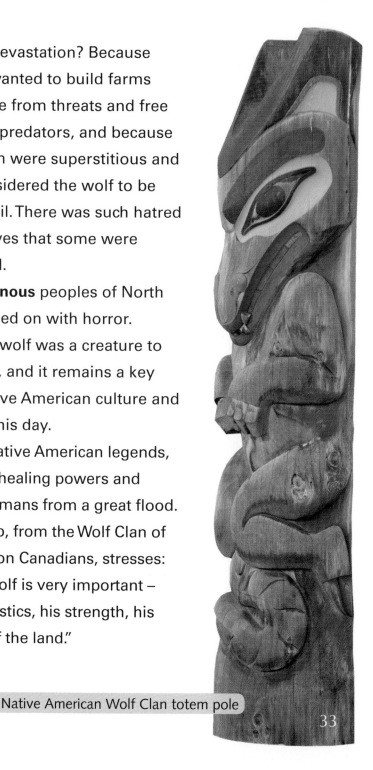

Native American Wolf Clan totem pole

WHERE WOLVES LIVE

Even though the worldwide population of Grey wolves
has increased in recent years, it's still much lower than it
was in the past. Together, the dark and light green areas on
this map show where wolves lived until the Middle Ages.
The dark green areas show where wolves can be
found today.

Changes in attitudes to wolves have led to the recent
global increase in their numbers. For example, in Poland,
the Grey wolf population once declined as a result of
the government actively encouraging wolf hunting.
This stopped in 1998, and now there are wolf packs in
most of Poland's forested areas.

Being very adaptable creatures, wolves can live in
a wide range of climates and habitats, from deserts and
plains to mountains and forests.

current range   historic range

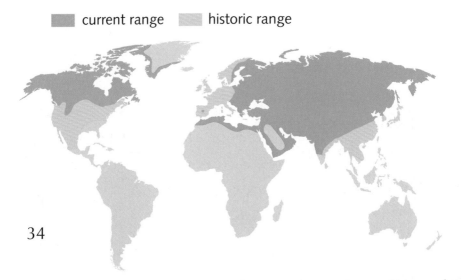

Wolf habitats

For wolves, the wilder and more **remote** the habitat is, the better. They are highly territorial animals, and their territories are often much larger than they actually need – up to hundreds of square kilometres. This allows them to have a plentiful supply

of prey. Like domestic dogs, they defend their territories by scenting with urine or by leaving dung.

Wolves dig underground dens to give birth and provide safe, dry places to bring up their cubs. They can also live in caves, or reuse previous dens, or even adapt the homes of creatures such as bears, foxes or badgers.

Unfortunately, you're not very likely to see a wolf in the wild – they don't wish to be spotted! There's even a Native American saying: "Once you see a wolf, it will have seen you a thousand times".

Wolf sanctuaries

For most people, the easiest way to see live wolves is to visit a zoo, a wildlife park or a sanctuary. In both Europe and America, there are now dedicated wolf centres.

UK Wolf Conservation Trust

One important wolf sanctuary in Britain is the UK Wolf Conservation Trust in West Berkshire. The roles of the trust include:

- conservation – rearing, caring for and **socialising** eight **ambassador** Grey wolves, five of which were born in England – the other three are Arctic wolves born in captivity in Canada

- education – raising the profile of wolves locally and globally, informing the public about wolves both through visits and through the Trust's magazine, *Wolf Print*

- fundraising for centres in other countries, including those that are focusing on endangered Red wolves and Ethiopian wolves.

International Wolf Centre

The International Wolf Centre is based in Minnesota, USA. It was set up by Dr David Mech, who has been one of the world's leading experts on wolves since 1958. As with the UK trust, one of the centre's main roles is educational – informing the public about the true nature of wolves.

The centre monitors and tracks a pack of Grey wolves that live on site, and gives visitors the opportunity to observe the wolves themselves, as well as go on wolf and wildlife field trips.

Wolf fact

Even in captivity, wolves never lose their fear of humans. However, wolves born and reared in sanctuaries can't properly function in the wild as they will not have the necessary skills and knowledge to survive.

Biologist David Mech with a sedated wolf

One of the most fun things to do if you visit a sanctuary
or centre – apart from having the great pleasure of actually
watching the wolves – is to try howling out loud. It's quite
likely that the wolves will respond to you. *A-WOOO!*

WOLF EXPERTS

Two of the most dedicated, high-profile wolf experts today are Jim and Jamie Dutcher. Together they have written a number of books on wolves, and Jim has produced award-winning

Jamie and Jim Dutcher

documentary films about wolves, as well as other wild animals.

The Dutchers built a 25-acre fenced area within which they created their own wolf pack, getting to know the wolves from birth and gaining their trust. They named the pack Sawtooth, after the Sawtooth Mountains where they were based in Idaho, US.

Despite extreme winters with ice, snow and freezing temperatures, the Dutchers lived in a tented camp alongside the wolves for six years. The Dutchers' research into the way wolf packs work has helped us to gain key insights into these previously mysterious creatures.

More recently, Jim and Jamie have established a charity organisation, Living with Wolves, that helps to promote wolf education worldwide. The couple now travel all over the USA running wolf education programmes.

Rewilding and the Wolf
Wolves in Yellowstone Park

In Yellowstone National Park in the US, wolves have been successfully reintroduced since the mid-1990s. Returning wolves or other species to the wild in this way is known as "rewilding", and can have many benefits, not just for the survival of that particular creature but for the whole **ecosystem** and the natural landscape.

YELLOWSTONE NATIONAL PARK

Yellowstone National Park

United States

In 1995, when the project in Yellowstone began, there were three wolf packs in the park, with 21 wolves altogether. By 2014, there were 11 packs of 104 wolves.

CREATING WOLF PACKS AT YELLOWSTONE

The wolves that were introduced to Yellowstone were taken from the wild, near Jasper National Park in Canada. The first batch was set loose from their pens into the park in March 1995, and further Canadian wolves were introduced between 1996 and 1997.

Before the wolves' release, the scientists involved deliberately created three new packs by putting pairs of parent wolves together with younger ones. They did this in three separate pens, in three different parts of Yellowstone. Within a day, each pack had bonded and the wolves knew their place within the group.

A SUCCESSFUL EXPERIMENT

In two out of the three packs, the parent wolves went on to have more cubs, but the other pair went their separate ways.

The wolves in Yellowstone have been monitored with radio collars since the beginning of the project. Early on, to help the wolves survive, the scientists would interact with and support them. In one case, they returned a female parent and her eight new pups to a pen after the male parent had been killed. They were released again a few months later.

THE EFFECTS OF REWILDING

It's been observed in Yellowstone Park that returning the wolf in this way has brought balance to the entire food chain, and helped trees, plants and other species of animals such as fox and beaver, and even improved the flow of the rivers.

Top predators such as wolves are vital to the health of the wild, as these carnivores reduce the numbers of herbivores such as deer, elk and boar. Left alone, the herbivores could grow too many in number and eat large quantities of essential grasses and plants. Some scientists believe that wolves also move herds of deer on, meaning that the deer won't take too much vegetation from one single area.

WOLF 06 FEMALE

One of the wolves in Yellowstone, known as "06 Female", became something of an international celebrity. She was observed bringing down a whole elk on her own, and also fending off grizzly bears to protect her pups. She wore a radio collar – and this is how we know that when she strayed from the park one day, she was shot down and killed by a hunter. In the state of Wyoming, it is illegal to kill wolves in the park, but not beyond. This story was reported by news stations worldwide, and wolf fans continue to remember the day of her death, 6th December 2012, for it has become her Annual Memorial Day.

Wolf 06 in Yellowstone Park

Dr Doug Smith

One of the world's leading wolf scientists, and a wolf fan since childhood, is Dr Doug Smith. He helped set up the Yellowstone National Wolf Restoration Project. Like Jim and Jamie Dutcher, he too has hand-reared wolf pups. Dr Smith strongly believes that "nature without wolves is not nature" – and every day of his life is dedicated to keeping wolves alive in the wild.

Dr Doug Smith of Yellowstone Park

REWILDING IN THE UK

Rewilding is currently happening in various places in the UK, including Wicken Fen Nature Reserve in Cambridgeshire, England and Alladale Wilderness Reserve in Scotland. Over the last ten years, a variety of mammals – including Red squirrel, beaver, wildcat and boar – have been successfully reintroduced at various sites in Scotland. All these mammals were once common all over Britain, and before the rewilding programmes they were previously low in numbers, if not extinct in the UK.

lynx

Red squirrel

Plans to reintroduce two other native top predators into Scotland, the wolf and the lynx, have met with fears and concerns that they would be a threat to people and to farm animals. Lynx, like wolves, are private creatures that pose no direct threat to humans. Lynx have recently and successfully been reintroduced into parts of Europe including Poland, Spain and Portugal.

Supporters of rewilding in Scotland believe that, due to regrowth of forested areas and increased deer populations, both the wolf and the lynx would enjoy vast habitats and plentiful prey if returned to the wild. They also believe these creatures would help to create a more balanced ecosystem for all plants, trees and animals in those areas.

beaver

Red deer

49

Conclusion: a new relationship

In the last 50 years, human attitudes towards the natural world have changed a great deal. In many countries, new laws have been passed to help protect wolves. Though most of us live in urban areas, we've become much more respectful of nature. Due to TV documentaries, novels, information books, websites and wolf sanctuaries, the reputation of the wolf has vastly improved.

Although in rural areas of Scandinavia and North America some hunters continue to seek out and kill wolves, the former "big bad wolf" of mythology is now generally a much-loved and revered creature.

When two animals of different species actively help each other, it's known as symbiosis. For example, ravens and wolves are symbiotic. Ravens will often show wolves where a source of food is, and once the wolves have found and killed their prey, the ravens will eat the remains of the carcass.

With the current rewilding programmes taking place, humans and wolves are beginning to forge a new, dynamic relationship. We are giving wolves large territories to live in, with plentiful prey, and in return, the wolves greatly improve the environment. For the first time in thousands of years, wolves and humans are once again working together, in a symbiosis of their own.

GLOSSARY

agility   ability to move quickly and gracefully

ambassador   wolves in captivity that represent their species

captivity   the opposite of the wild, when animals are confined

canid   the family wolves belong to, which includes foxes, coyotes, dingoes, jackals and pet dogs

climates   the usual sorts of weather in particular places

coyotes   canids native to Central and North America

cougars   large, North American wild cats

descendants   animals that come from a particular ancestor

domesticated   creatures bred or trained to need the care of human beings

ecosystem   all the living creatures – plants and animals – within a certain area

habitats   the natural environments of animals

hemisphere   the world can be split into two main sections – the northern and southern hemispheres, divided at the equator

herbivores   animals that eat only plants

indigenous   coming from and living in a particular area

lynx   a form of wild cat

mammals   warm-blooded animals that have backbones and hair or fur, and feed milk to their young

nutrition   food that is vital for growth and health

primates   mammals, including chimps, gorillas, monkeys and humans, that walk on two legs

provoked	made angry
remote	far from towns and cities
rodents	four-legged mammals with large front teeth – such as mice, rats, squirrels and hamsters
scenting	when a wolf marks its territory, often with urine or dung
socialising	the process when an animal from an early age is encouraged to mix with humans
terrain	land or landscape
wean	give food other than a mother's milk to young

INDEX

A WOLF TIMELINE

first Grey wolves appear a million years ago in Asia

foot and paw prints in Chauvet Cave, France, from 26,000 years ago, of a boy and wolf travelling together

miacids – prehistoric carnivores – appear 62 million years ago

domestic dogs appear 30,000+ years ago

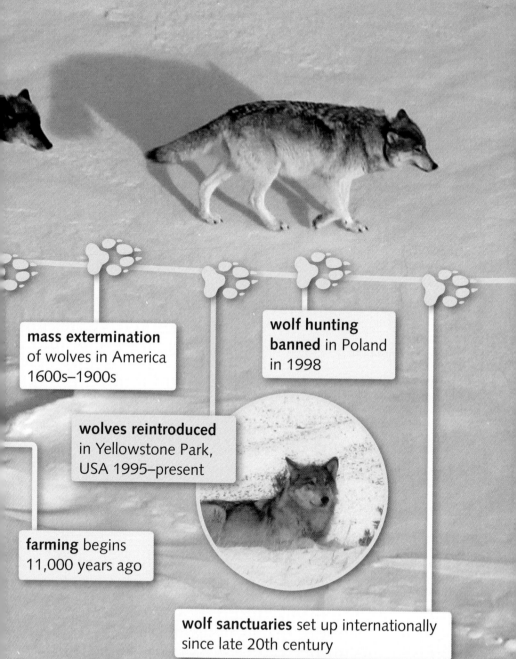

mass extermination of wolves in America 1600s–1900s

wolf hunting banned in Poland in 1998

wolves reintroduced in Yellowstone Park, USA 1995–present

farming begins 11,000 years ago

wolf sanctuaries set up internationally since late 20th century

Ideas for reading

Written by Clare Dowdall, PhD
Lecturer and Primary Literacy Consultant

Reading objectives:
- ask questions to improve understanding
- summarise the main ideas drawn from more than one paragraph, identifying key details that support the main ideas
- explain and discuss understanding, including through formal presentations and debates, maintaining a focus on the topic and using notes where necessary

Spoken language objectives:
- ask relevant questions to extend their understanding and knowledge
- give well-structured descriptions, explanations and narratives for different purposes

Curriculum links: Science – evolution and inheritance

Resources: whiteboards and pens, ICT, pens and paper or ICT for poster making

Build a context for reading
- Collect children's ideas about wolves and their behaviour on a whiteboard.
- Look at the front cover and read the blurb. Challenge children to suggest what being misunderstood means, and how wolves might be misunderstood.
- Read through the contents together. Check that children can read the word "reputation" and discuss what a reputation is, using familiar examples.

Understand and apply reading strategies
- Using the whiteboard ideas, work with children to raise questions that can be answered by reading. Note the questions for later.